Where is Marshmallow?

by

Kathryn Lynn Seifert

illustrated by Ann Murray and Jean Weir

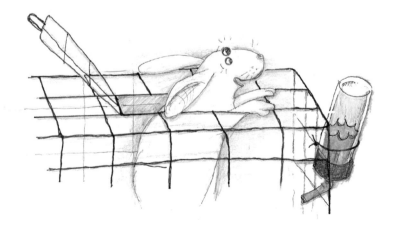

For my family and the best teacher I know, our daughter, Amber.
Love, Mom

Children's books by Kathryn Lynn Seifert and illustrated by Ann Murray

Penelope: The Adventures of a Penny

Hank the Hanger

Ellie's Room

Littleleaf Linden

Educational Games:

Word Dissection

State It!

"Maggie, time to get up." Mom gently prodded me and then kissed my cheek.

My eyes flashed open. "Today! Today is the day our class gets our pet bunny, Marshmallow, Mom!" I whipped my covers off, jumped out of bed, got dressed, and rushed to the kitchen table.

I began gulping down my cereal.
I knew that being on time for the
bus would be easy today.

When I arrived at school, my best friend, Susan, was waiting at our classroom window. Alongside of her was Charlie, her seeing-eye dog.

I ran up to Susan. As soon as I spotted Marshmallow, I began describing him to Susan. I told Susan that Marshmallow's fur was white and fluffy like freshly fallen snow. I described how the insides of his ears were bright pink, just like bubblegum.

Susan smiled. I knew that she was painting a picture of Marshmallow in her head. I often help Susan see things by describing them to her. Susan can't see very well. My friend Susan has a visual impairment.

As my classmates and I waited out-
side the classroom window, it appeared
that everyone was as excited as Susan
and I were! We grew even more excited
when Mrs. Tanner began filling up
Marshmallow's food dish. Mrs. Tanner
heard the commotion at the window,
turned around, and smiled.

6

R-R-R-I-I-N-N-G-G!! We all bolted toward the class-room door and lined up quickly. Mrs. Tanner instructed us to go directly to our seats. She could tell by the way we were sitting that we couldn't wait to pet Marshmallow!

So, Mrs. Tanner said that she'd first call up those who were working neatly and quietly on their morning work. We got to our morning work right away. Joey was the first to glance over at Marshmallow's cage.

Immediately Joey yelled, "Mrs. Tanner! Where is Marshmallow?"

9

"Well, I think our new friend wants to check out our classroom! Hmmm... where is he?" Mrs. Tanner muttered.

Mrs. Tanner set out a plate of rabbit pellets. "If you see Marshmallow munching, let me know and I will scoop him up," she stated.

The whole day passed by and still no Marshmallow. Before we knew it, it was 3:00 p.m. and time to go home.

The next day, the school principal, Mr. Mason, made a school-wide announcement. "All classrooms, please keep an eye out for Mrs. Tanner's 3rd grade bunny, Marshmallow."

There was a buzz of excitement throughout school that day. Eyes were peering this way and that, and many of us shared our ideas on how we would capture Marshmallow.

On the bus ride home, a third grader named Jeremy, told everyone sitting near him about rabbits. I was amazed at how much he knew about them! He excitedly looked off into the distance as he rattled off many interesting facts and opinions about rabbits.

Fast runners

Pretty pink eyes, nose, and mouth

Good sense of smell

Mmmm... veggies

When it was time for Jeremy to get off of the bus, he jumped up and zoomed off. His mother was at the end of their driveway, just as she always is. If she doesn't meet Jeremy each day, he may wander away. Jeremy gets easily distracted... he often wants to check out the neighbor's dog or the tree fort in the woods. Our friend, Jeremy, has autism.

During snack time the following day, Mrs. Tanner wrote down all of our ideas on how to capture Marshmallow. I shared with the class what Jeremy told us about rabbits. They like pineapple, Romaine lettuce, raisins, and lots more. That's all I could remember. I knew Jeremy could remember a lot more, though!

cucumbers

Children volunteered to bring in the treats that Jeremy said bunnies like. We left trails of these treats throughout our classroom.

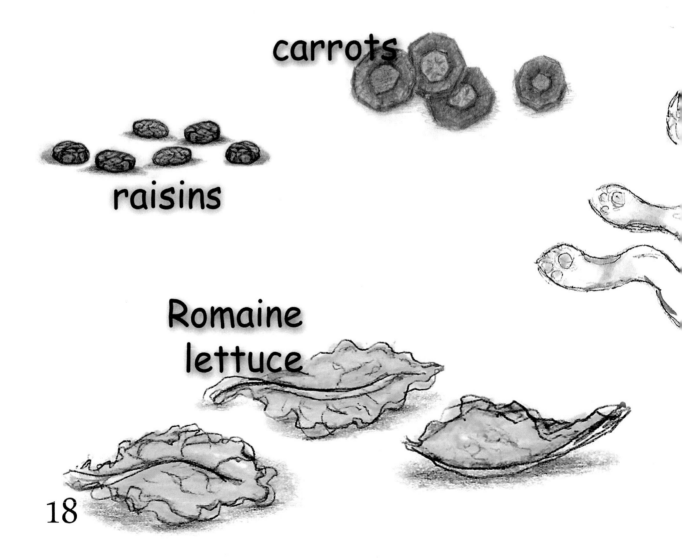
carrots

raisins

Romaine lettuce

Another day went by... there were still no signs of Marshmallow. Chris, a friendly boy in second grade, had been absent for a couple of days. Chris heard about Marshmallow. Smiling, Chris cheered, "Let's find Marshmallow!"

"We hope we will," responded Chris's teacher, Mr. Baker. Chris had to leave to go to another classroom for his special math class where he works with another teacher. He learns differently from other kids his age. Our friend, Chris, has Down syndrome.

On Friday, Jeremy climbed the monkey bars. He announced that his toy dinosaurs in the classroom had been knocked down. As part of Jeremy's autism, he likes to line them up each day. He gets upset when anyone moves them.

Jeremy started to cry. A boy with black curly hair cried out, "Hey, maybe the bunny knocked them down!"

Everyone on the monkey bars gathered around... "Yeah, I bet it was! Let's tell Mr. Baker. Jeremy, Marshmallow must be in your classroom!" When the bell rang, they told their teacher about Jeremy's dinosaurs.

Later that day, Susan and I were in Jeremy's classroom meeting with our reading group.

Suddenly, Susan tapped me and whispered, "Maggie, I hear a crunching sound over there!"

I spun around and saw Marshmallow's fluffy white tail disappear behind the bookshelf. "Susan, it's Marshmallow!" I screeched. Since Susan can't see very well, she depends on her hearing a lot. Her hearing is VERY good!

"Maggie, I hear it again... over by the bean bag," Susan exclaimed. I peered behind the bean bag, and there was Marshmallow! He was happily munching on a carrot.

By now, Mr. Baker and the rest of the class were looking at me reaching out to Marshmallow. He was trapped in the corner.

I put my hand out, and he hopped over to smell it. That was my moment to quickly grab him!

When Mr. Baker walked us back to our classroom, I carried Marshmallow. I gently slid my hand under Marshmallow's belly and used my other hand to support his back legs. I held him close to my body.

Walking into the classroom, I exclaimed, "Marshmallow's back!" Everyone cheered! Mrs. Tanner scooped him out of my arms and put him in his cage. We all watched. We noticed that Marshmallow was shaking. I think that all of the excitement scared him.

Mrs. Tanner asked if Susan and I would go to the office and let Principal Mason know that Marshmallow had been found.

When Principal Mason announced that Marshmallow had been found, Chris asked his teacher if he could come to our classroom.

Mr. Baker smiled and said, "Absolutely, Chris!" Chris knocked on our door. He asked if he could hold our bunny. Mrs. Tanner knew about Chris's gentle ways and agreed that he would be just the right student to comfort Marshmallow. "Come on in and sit in our bean bag chair, Chris." Marshmallow rested his head on Chris's arm and slowly closed his eyes.

31

Marshmallow was home, and we all helped rescue him!